P9-DBY-919

For Geraldine, Joe, Naomi,
Eddie, Laura and Isaac
M.R.

For Amelia
H.O.

First Aladdin Paperbacks edition January 2003

Text copyright © 1989 by Michael Rosen
Illustrations copyright © 1989 by Helen Oxenbury

First published in Great Britain in 1989
by Walker Books Ltd. London
Published by arrangement with Walker Books Ltd.

ALADDIN PAPERBACKS
An imprint of Simon & Schuster
Children's Publishing Division
1230 Avenue of the Americas
New York, NY 10020

All rights reserved, including the right of
reproduction in whole or in part in any form.

Also available in a Margaret K. McElderry Books for Young Readers edition.
The text of this book was set in Veronan Light Educational

Manufactured in China
30 29 28 27 26 25 24 23 22

The Library of Congress has cataloged the hardcover edition as follows:

Rosen, Michael, date
We're going on a bear hunt/retold by Michael Rosen; illustrated by Helen Oxenbury
p. cm.
Summary: Brave bear hunters go through grass, a river, mud, and other obstacles
before the inevitable encounter with the bear forces a headlong retreat.
[1. Bears—Fiction. 2. Hunting—Fiction]. I. Oxenbury, Helen, ill. II. title
PZ7.R71867We 1989 [E]—dc19   88-13338 CP AC

978-0-689-85349-4 (Aladdin pbk.)
0-689-85349-1 (Aladdin pbk.)

0718 WAL

We're Going on a Bear Hunt

Retold by

Michael Rosen

Illustrated by

Helen Oxenbury

ALADDIN PAPERBACKS

New York London Toronto Sydney Singapore

We're going on a bear hunt.

We're going to catch a big one.

What a beautiful day!

We're not scared.

Oh-oh! Grass!
Long, wavy grass.
We can't go over it.
We can't go under it.

Oh, no!
We've got to go through it!

Swishy swashy!
Swishy swashy!
Swishy swashy!

We're going on a bear hunt.

We're going to catch a big one.

What a beautiful day!

We're not scared.

Oh-oh! A river!

A deep, cold river.

We can't go over it.

We can't go under it.

Oh, no!

We've got to go through it!

Splash splosh!
Splash splosh!
Splash splosh!

We're going on a bear hunt.

We're going to catch a big one.

What a beautiful day!

We're not scared.

Oh-oh! Mud!
Thick, oozy mud.
We can't go over it.
We can't go under it.

Oh, no!
We've got to go through it!

Squelch squerch!
Squelch squerch!
Squelch squerch!

We're going on a bear hunt.

We're going to catch a big one.

What a beautiful day!

We're not scared.

Oh-oh! A forest!
A big, dark forest.
We can't go over it.
We can't go under it.

Oh, no!
We've got to go through it!

Stumble trip!
Stumble trip!
Stumble trip!

We're going on a bear hunt.

We're going to catch a big one.

What a beautiful day!

We're not scared.

Oh-oh! A snowstorm!

A swirling, whirling snowstorm.

We can't go over it.

We can't go under it.

Oh, no!

We've got to go through it!

Hoooo woooo!

Hoooo woooo!

Hoooo woooo!

We're going on a bear hunt.

We're going to catch a big one.

What a beautiful day!

We're not scared.

Oh-oh! A cave!
A narrow, gloomy cave.
We can't go over it.
We can't go under it.

Oh, no!
We've got to go through it!

Tiptoe!

    Tiptoe!

        Tiptoe!

WHAT'S THAT?

One shiny wet nose!

Two big furry ears!

Two big goggly eyes!

IT'S A BEAR!!!!

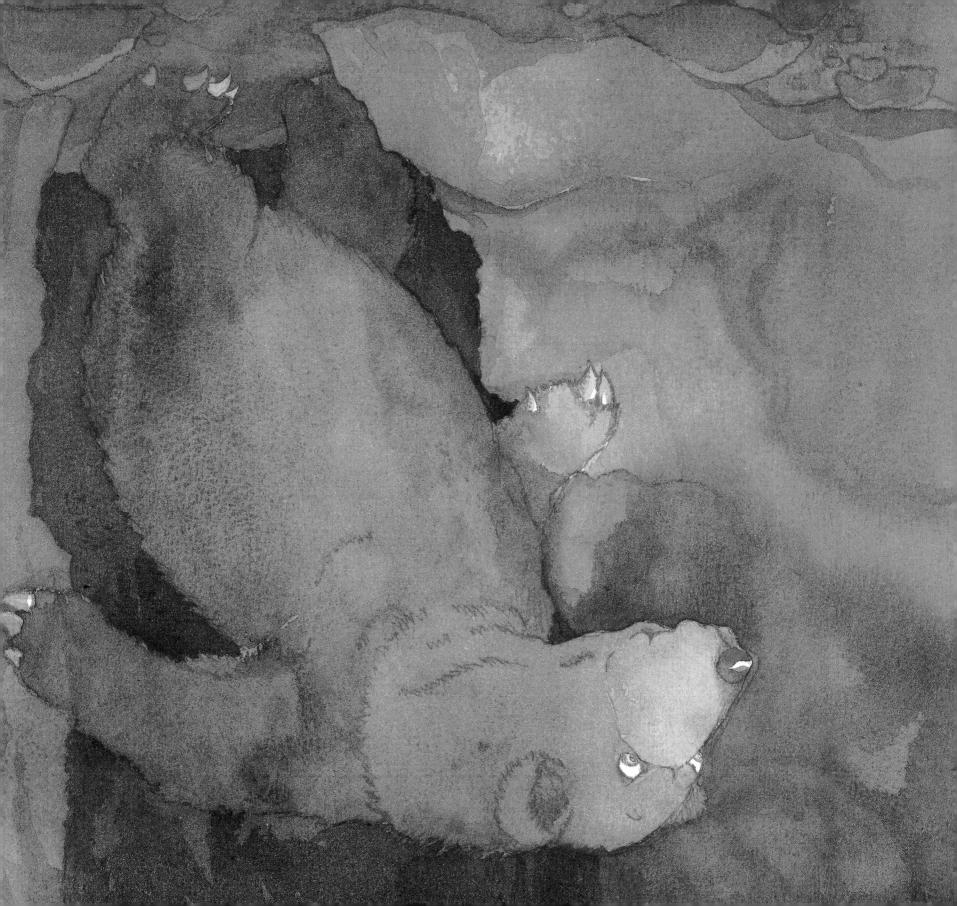

Quick! Back through the cave! Tiptoe! Tiptoe! Tiptoe!

Back through the snowstorm! Hoooo woooo! Hoooo woooo!

Back through the forest! Stumble trip! Stumble trip! Stumble trip!

Back through the mud! Squelch squerch! Squelch squerch!

Back through the river! Splash splosh! Splash splosh! Splash splosh!

Back through the grass! Swishy swashy! Swishy swashy!

Get to our front door.

Open the door.

Up the stairs.

Oh, no!

We forgot to shut the door.

Back downstairs.

Shut the door.

Back upstairs.

Into the bedroom.

Into bed.

Under the covers.

We're not going on

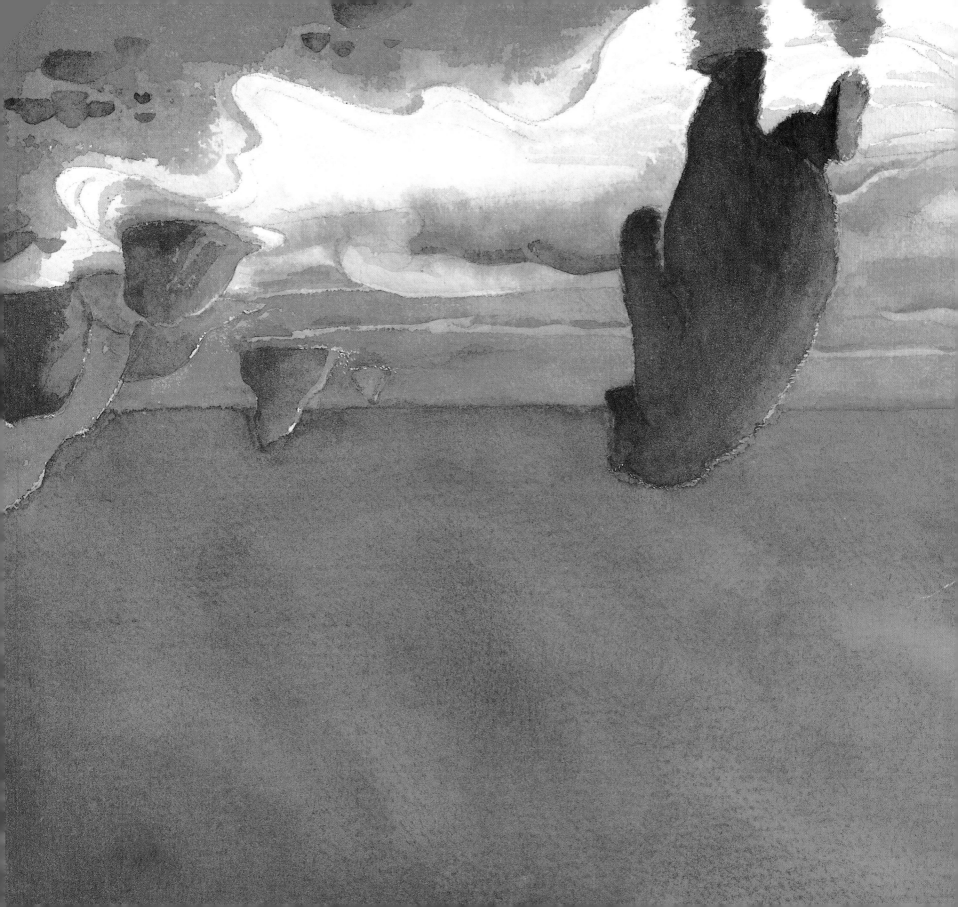